# Snow White

Once there was a beautiful and kind-hearted queen who lived in an old castle. One day, while embroidering, she pricked herself.

'If only I could have a baby,' she thought, 'with lips as red as blood and hair as black as ebony.'

A short time later her wish came true. A baby girl was born, and the queen called her Snow White. Sadly, after giving birth, the kind-hearted queen died.

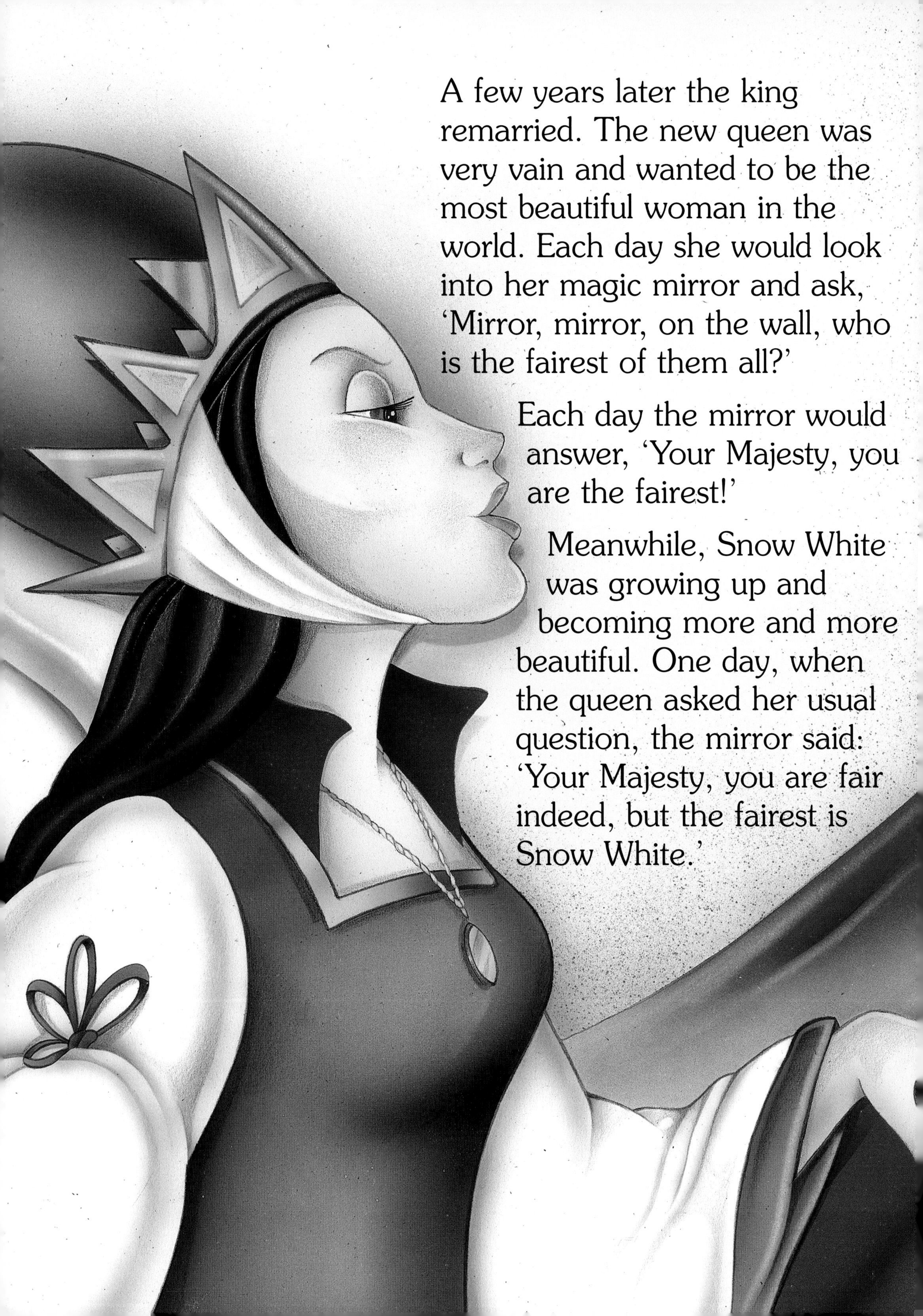

A few years later the king remarried. The new queen was very vain and wanted to be the most beautiful woman in the world. Each day she would look into her magic mirror and ask, 'Mirror, mirror, on the wall, who is the fairest of them all?'

Each day the mirror would answer, 'Your Majesty, you are the fairest!'

Meanwhile, Snow White was growing up and becoming more and more beautiful. One day, when the queen asked her usual question, the mirror said: 'Your Majesty, you are fair indeed, but the fairest is Snow White.'

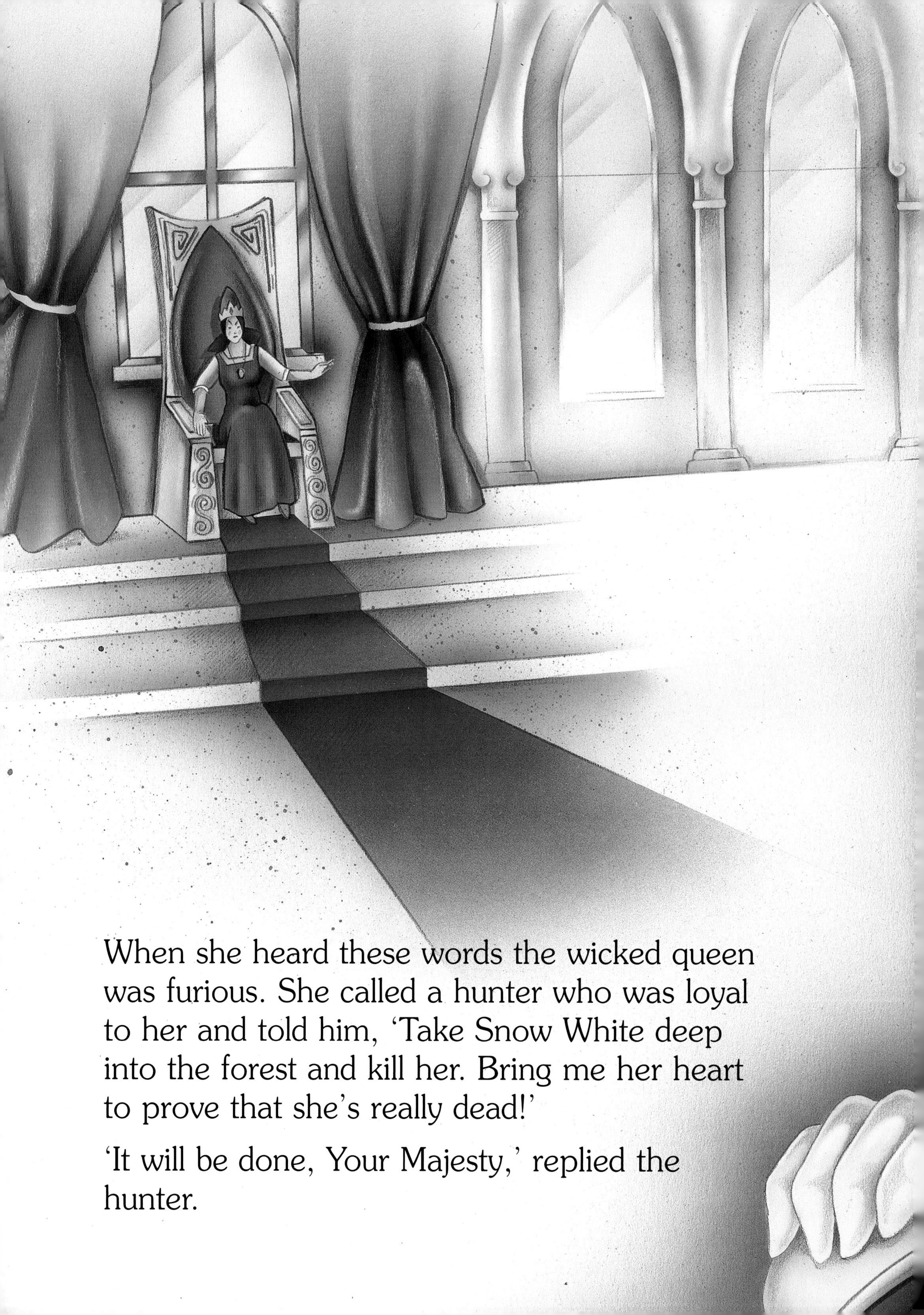

When she heard these words the wicked queen was furious. She called a hunter who was loyal to her and told him, 'Take Snow White deep into the forest and kill her. Bring me her heart to prove that she's really dead!'

'It will be done, Your Majesty,' replied the hunter.

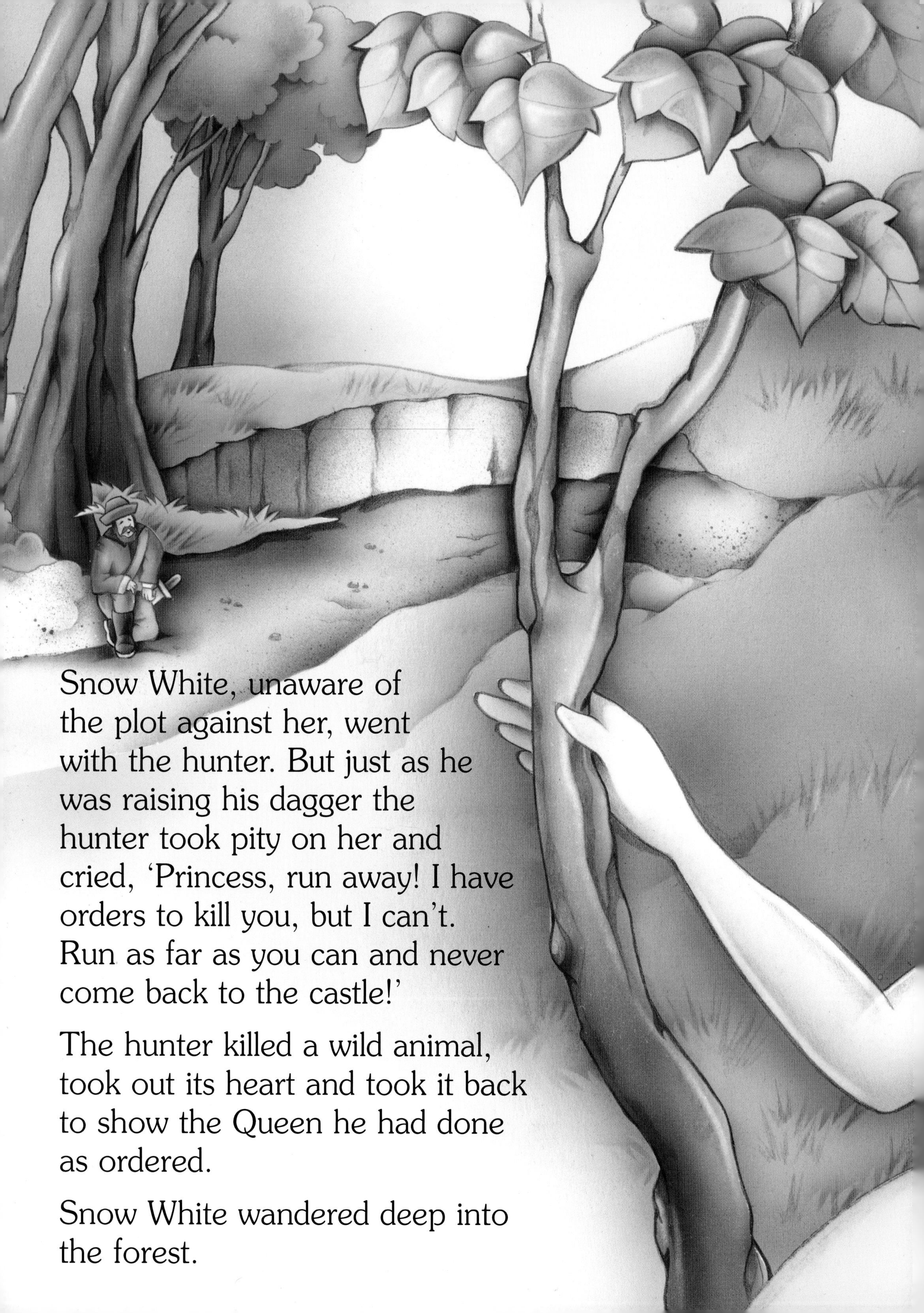

Snow White, unaware of the plot against her, went with the hunter. But just as he was raising his dagger the hunter took pity on her and cried, 'Princess, run away! I have orders to kill you, but I can't. Run as far as you can and never come back to the castle!'

The hunter killed a wild animal, took out its heart and took it back to show the Queen he had done as ordered.

Snow White wandered deep into the forest.

She was all alone and lost and very frightened. After walking a long time she saw, in the distance, a pretty little cottage.

‘It’s *ever* so tiny! Who could live there?’ Snow White went up and knocked softly on the door. No-one answered. She knocked again, and this time the door, which wasn’t shut, opened by itself.

Walking in, she saw a table set with seven little bowls and seven little spoons. Snow White was so hungry she decided to have something to eat. Ever so cautiously she tasted some of her mysterious hosts' supper. Then she went to see the rest of the house.

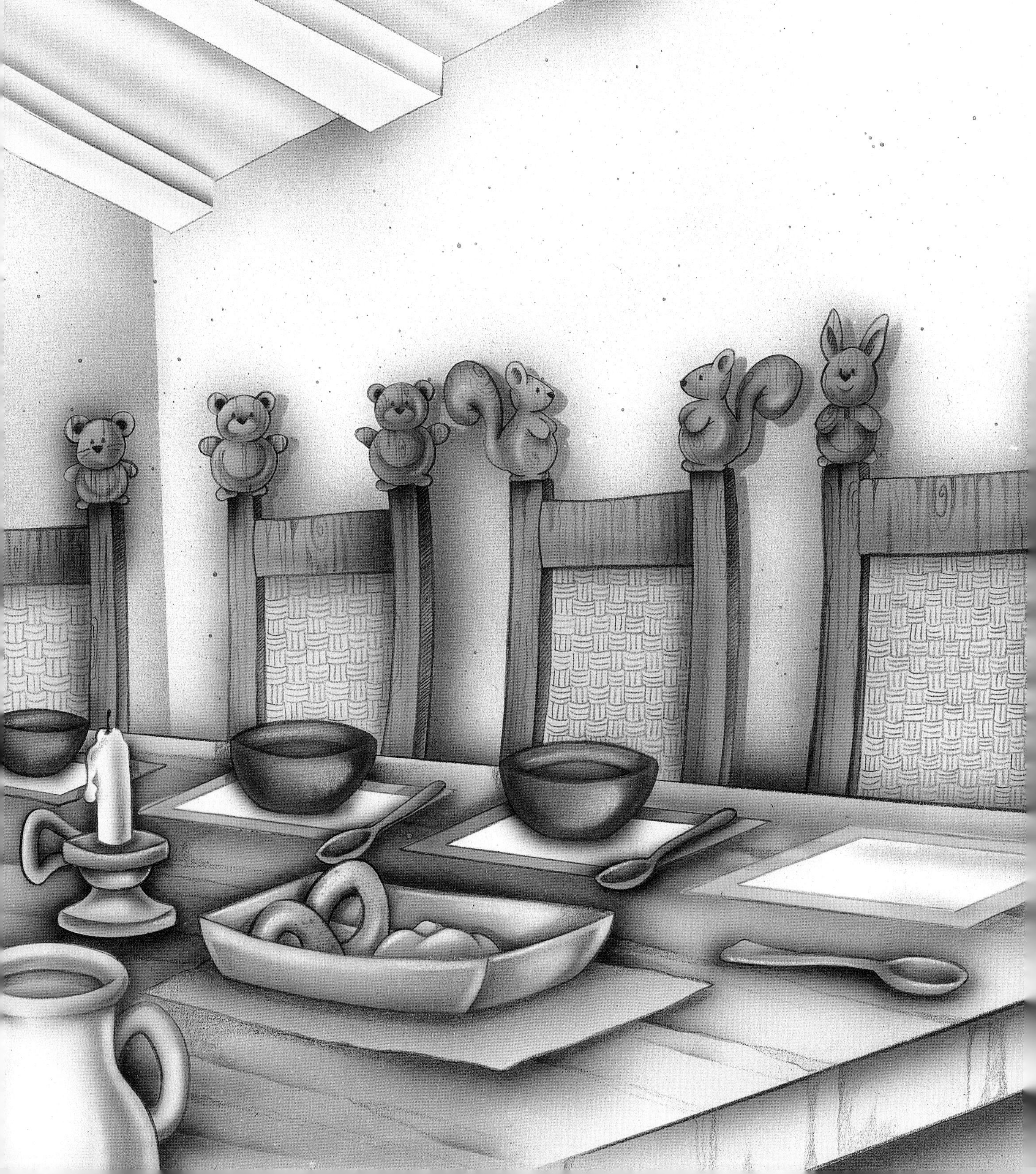

She walked into a bedroom where there were seven identical little beds next to one another. Overcome with tiredness, she lay down across the little beds and fell asleep.

In the evening the little owners of the cottage came home. They were seven dwarfs who went to work every day at a mine, digging for precious metals. They quickly realised someone had been sampling their supper.

Then their astonishment grew: 'Look over here!' said one of them. The dwarfs rushed over to see a beautiful girl lying across their beds.

'She's so beautiful! Who is she?' they murmured. Snow White opened her eyes, looked around in amazement and greeted the little dwarfs with a sweet smile.

'Who are you? What's your name?' they asked together.

The girl told them her sad tale. Frowning sternly, the dwarfs said, 'Your life is in danger!'

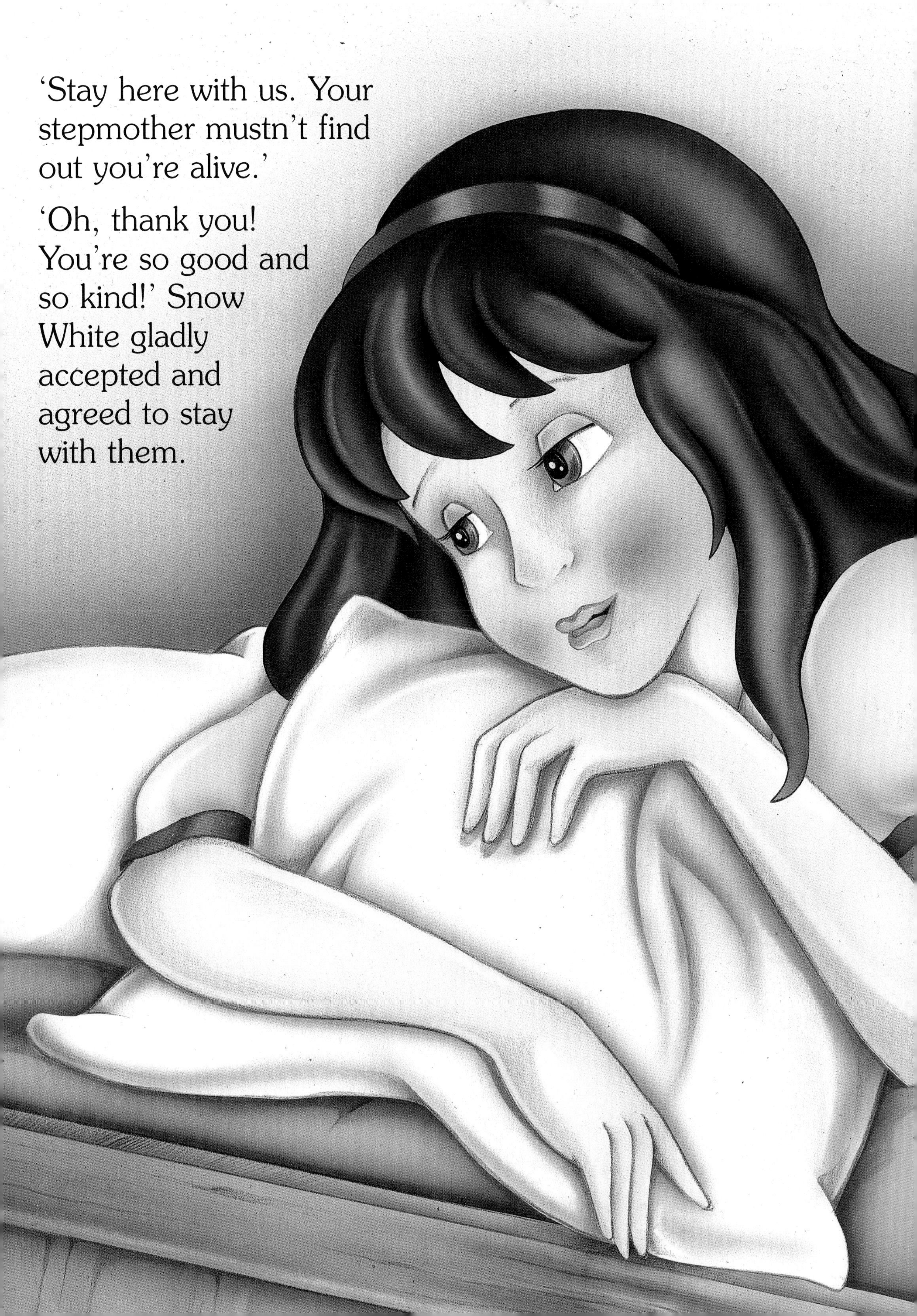

'Stay here with us. Your stepmother mustn't find out you're alive.'

'Oh, thank you! You're so good and so kind!' Snow White gladly accepted and agreed to stay with them.

The next morning the dwarfs took their tools and went off to work. As they waved goodbye to Snow White they were careful to warn her, 'Remember: don't open the door to anyone!'

Meanwhile the wicked queen, using her magic mirror, had found Snow White's hiding place. She went down into the castle dungeons and dipped an apple in strong poison.

Next she disguised herself as an old woman. 'With this mask and these old clothes I'm unrecognisable.'

She went to the seven dwarfs' house. 'Scarves, ribbons! Pretty, coloured ribbons for sale...' she called.

Innocent Snow White, out of curiosity, opened the door.

'Hello, my dear,' said the queen. 'Would you like to buy this lovely ribbon?'

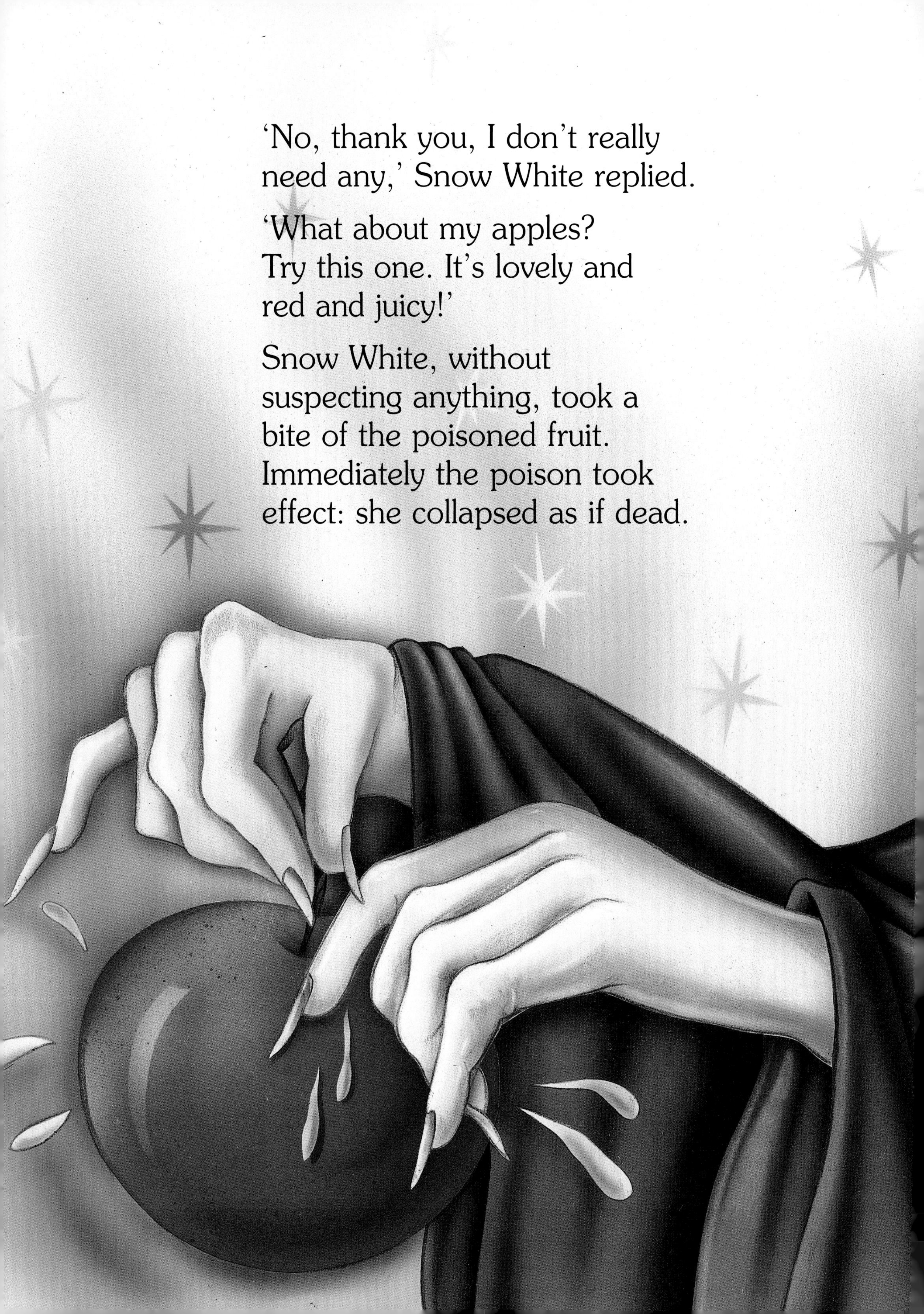

'No, thank you, I don't really need any,' Snow White replied.

'What about my apples? Try this one. It's lovely and red and juicy!'

Snow White, without suspecting anything, took a bite of the poisoned fruit. Immediately the poison took effect: she collapsed as if dead.

The evil queen burst out laughing. 'Well, now I am the fairest of them all!' she cried – and left.

The little creatures of the forest approached Snow White. They couldn't believe she was dead!

Meanwhile, back at the castle, the stepmother stood before the magic mirror; but it said:

'Your Majesty, Snow White is no more, but from now on your face will be as ugly as your heart.'

The queen took off her mask and, seeing how horrible she looked, ran away, never to be seen again.

That night the dwarfs returned home. They were whistling happily, knowing that Snow White would be waiting for them. They were horrified when they saw the young girl lying lifeless on the ground.

They tried everything to revive Snow White, but there was nothing they could do. 'Poor Snow White! It was the evil queen! We should have been more careful,' they sobbed.

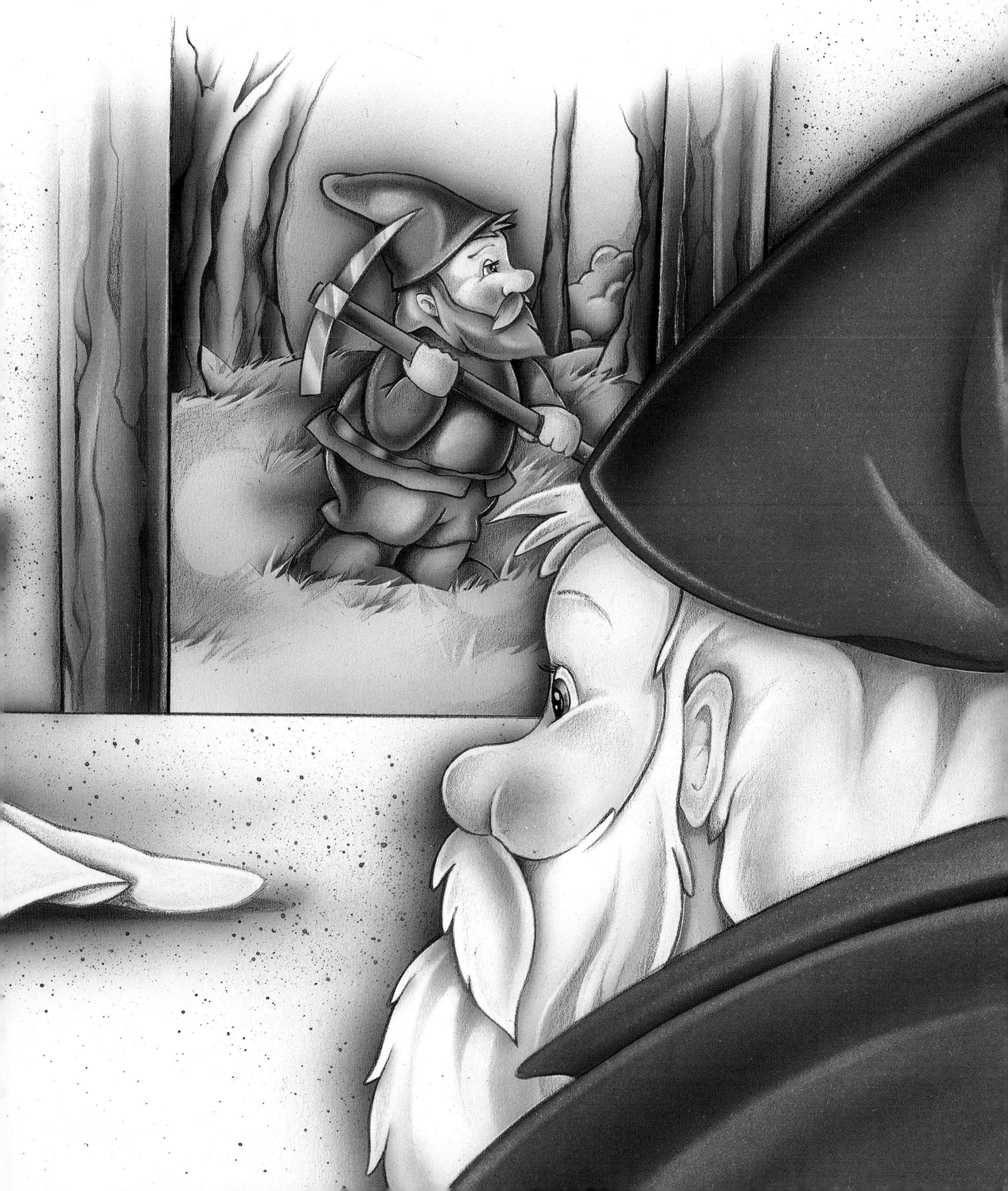

‘She’s so beautiful the whole world needs to see her!’ said the littlest of the dwarfs. So they decided to lay her on a crystal bed in the forest. The dwarfs stayed by her side and didn’t leave her for a single moment. The girl looked like she was sleeping.

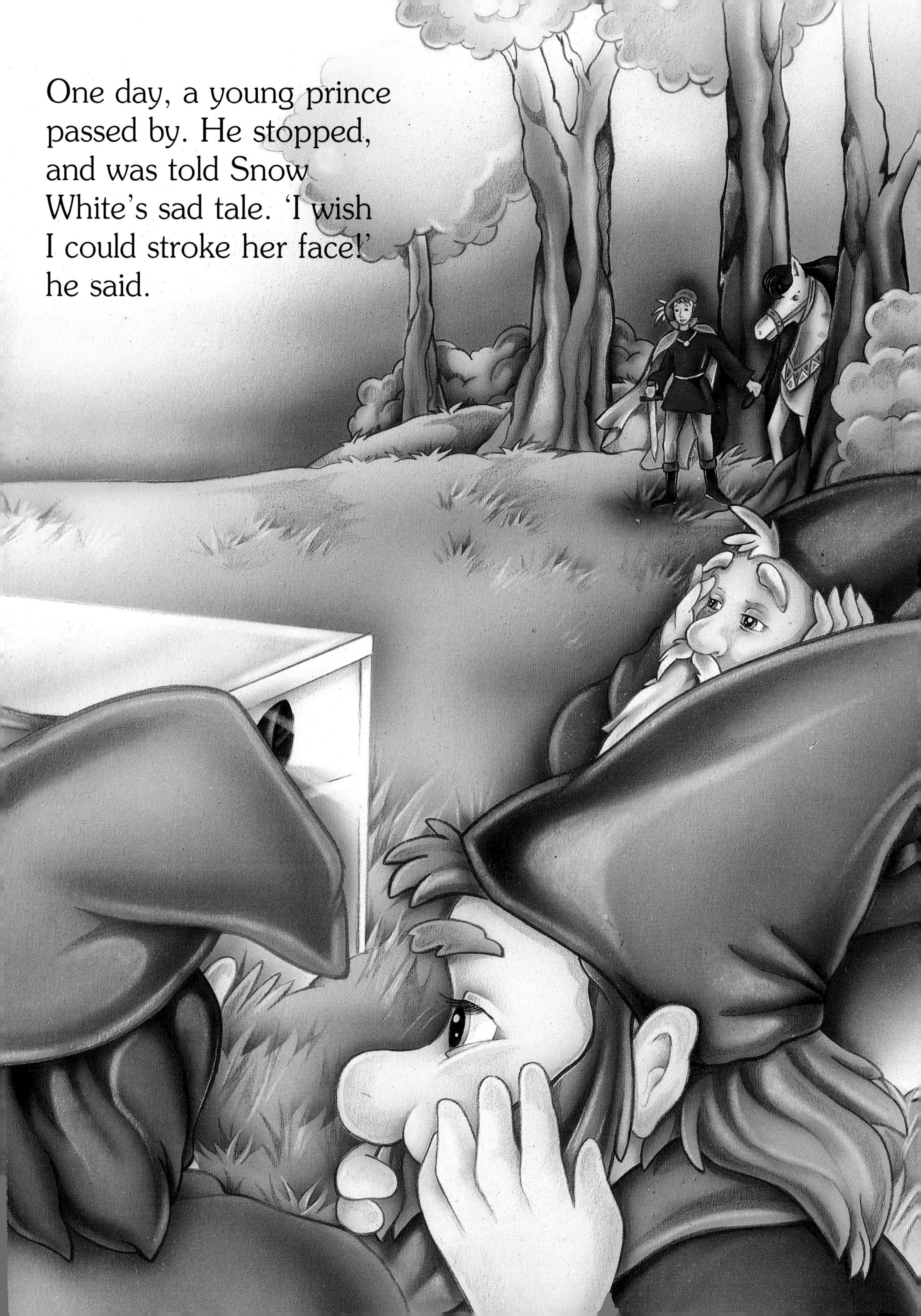

One day, a young prince passed by. He stopped, and was told Snow White's sad tale. 'I wish I could stroke her face!' he said.

Moved, he took Snow White in his arms, brought his lips to hers and kissed her.

Suddenly the girl opened her eyes and murmured, 'Where am I? What happened to me?'

The prince gently explained what had happened and asked her, 'Will you be my princess?'

Snow White accepted his proposal. The seven dwarfs were invited to the wedding. They had lost Snow White all over again, but this time they were happy.

decay and ends once dust has returned to dust, the conversation of Shoshe and Shmul-Leibele ends only as their eternal life begins: "Yes, the brief years of turmoil and temptation had come to an end. Shmul-Leibele and Shoshe had reached the true world. Man and wife grew silent. In the stillness they heard the flapping of wings, a quiet singing. An angel of God had come to guide Shmul-Leibele the tailor and his wife, Shoshe, into Paradise" (243).

In Singer's work, redemption is personal rather than communal and secular rather than religious. But it echoes those redemptive possibilities and at times, as in "Short Friday," points directly to them. Singer shows that through love one forms a measure of human community, and he reveals sexual love to be suggestive of the ecstasy of cosmic redemption, rendered in the Kabbalah by the imagery of the sexual union of *Ein-Sof* and his exiled bride.

# *Notes*
# *Bibliography*
# *Index*

# Notes

## 1. Analogues of Exile: A Hidden God and an Empty Cosmos

1. Friedman 3–36 provides an in-depth discussion of Job and Prometheus as essential figures precursory to modern images of humankind.
2. Job, as Murray Krieger writes of his "ethical man," undergoes "a cosmic 'shock,'" waking up to find himself, like Kafka's K, "irrevocably arrested 'without having done anything wrong.'" He discovers "suddenly that the neatly ordered and easily enacted worldly rights and wrongs of his ethical assumptions are utterly inadequate to the data of his moral experience" (12–13).
3. The Lurianic Kabbalah, which is a primary source of inspiration for Singer, is considered extensively in chap. 2. It posits a curtain or wall between the realm of the divine and the created world order—another image of the exile of humankind from the transcendent. See Scholem, *Major Trends* 272–73.
4. Singer is well acquainted with Maimonides, alluding to him frequently throughout his work.
5. See Burgin's discussion of "the problem of not knowing" which is at the heart of Singer's "Sly Modernism."

## 2. Belief and Disbelief: The Kabbalic Basis of Singer's Secular Vision

1. Singer's world view is, indeed, deeply rooted in the profoundly God-filled folk culture of his childhood. Born into a distinguished line of rabbis, he grew up immersed in the legends and treatises of Hasidism, a mystical revival movement which flowered in Eastern Europe in the eighteenth century. Led by the saintly Rabbi Israel ben Eliezer, the *Baal Shem Tov*, Hasidism was characterized by joy and fervor in religious expression. It arose quite separately from, and oftentimes in opposition to, the eighteenth-century Jewish Enlightenment, which sought, among other things, to purge Judaism of its folkish elements.

Hasidic literature consists partly of collections of legends, biographical anecdotes, and folktales, which have been popularized in the West by Martin Buber's editions. It also includes a substantial body of theoretical works based on the Kabbalah, the fundamental work of Jewish mysticism which attempts to discover the secrets of creation and the nature of God.

Gershom Scholem, the great scholar of Jewish mysticism, provides a corrective to Buber's emphasis on the legends and tales of Hasidism to the neglect of the Kabbalic literature, contending that such emphasis has led to the widespread misconception that Hasidism is a popular mysticism of unlettered people. It is interesting to note the parallel misconception often held of Singer, which views him as a natural storyteller who has few, if any, theoretical concerns. Such a view can lead readers to resist any discussions of the analytical nature of his texts. But Singer inherited from his Hasidic background both the simple joy of telling stories and the speculative proclivities of the Kabbalic theoreticians. See Singer, *Reaches of Heaven* and *Hasidim.* For discussions of Hasidism, see Scholem, *Major Trends* 88–118, 326–30; Sachar 72–80; Buber, *Origin and Meaning.* For Buber's collection of Hasidic literature, see *Hasidim* and *Rabbi Nachman.* For a fine selection of Hasidic literature, complete with indexes of sources and motifs, see Ben-Amos and Mintz. For Scholem's discussion of Buber, see "Martin Buber's Interpretation of Hasidism," *Messianic Idea* 228–50. Singer makes clear his view that Hasidism was "rooted in the Kabbalah" (*Hasidim* 16).

2. For an extensive discussion of the historical development of the Kabbalah, see Scholem, *Kabbalah* chap. 2. Bloom offers another contemporary rendition of the Kabbalah as a basis for his literary criticism. See also Riddel's review essay of the above.
3. The *Zohar* was traditionally assumed to be the work of Simeon ben Yohai who taught in Palestine in the second century, but more likely, modern scholars contend, it was composed in the late thirteenth century by the Spanish Kabbalist Moses de Leon. For a complete translation of the *Zohar,* see Sperling and Simon; for selections, see Scholem, *Zohar.*
4. For a discussion of the Safed circle, see Scholem, *Kabbalah* chap. 2.

5. For further discussions by Scholem of *tzimtzum* and emanation, see *On the Kabbalah*, especially 110–17; *Messianic Idea*, especially chap. 2; *Kabbalah* 128–40. See also "Schöpfung aus Nichts" and *Major Trends* 260–68.
6. For other readings of "Gimpel," see especially Pinsker; Wisse 58–69; Paul N. Siegel.
7. I am indebted to Dr. Lois A. Cuddy, Professor of English, The University of Rhode Island, for this insight.
8. The *Sefer Yezirah*, once thought to be the work of the patriarch Abraham, predates the *Zohar* and was probably composed between the third and sixth centuries. Stenring provides an accessible translation.
9. See Trachtenberg for an extensive treatment of such magic, especially chaps. 7–9, app. 1.

## 3. Demonic Dimensions of Exile: Reading the Short Stories

1. As Gittleman writes, "The process of telling . . . is the primary reality which defines Singer's short fiction" ("Dybbukianism" 250).
2. *Gilgul*, the Hebrew term for transmigration of souls, reincarnation, or metempsychosis, and *ibbur*, which involves the entry of one soul into that of another person, occur often in Singer's work and are yet other forms of exile. As Scholem writes: "The exile of the body in outward history has its parallel in the exile of the soul in its migrations from embodiment to embodiment, from one form of being to another. The doctrine of metempsychosis as the exile of the soul acquired unprecedented popularity among the Jewish masses of the generations following the Lurianic period" (*On the Kabbalah* 116). See also Scholem, *Kabbalah* 157, 344ff., 348–49, *Major Trends* 250; Franck 129.
3. Jonas suggests this phrase when discussing the myriad layers of demonic realms in folk religion (51–54).
4. See Scholem, *On the Kabbalah* 154, *Kabbalah* 122–28, 320–26, 349ff., 356ff., Gaster 370; Trachtenberg 25. Demonology, it should be noted, is not an integral part of mainstream Judaism. Scholem explains that "Jewish philosophers dismissed [the problem of evil and the demonic] as a pseudo-problem, while to

the Kabbalists it became one of the chief motives of their thinking" (*On the Kabbalah* 99).

5. Scholem writes, "the root of all evil is already latent in the act of *Tsimtsum*" (*Major Trends* 263). See 260–67 for further discussion. See also Scholem, *On the Kabbalah* 92–95; Schaya 48ff.
6. Singer's discussion of seeing and blindness is suggestive of similarities between Kabbalism and Gnosticism, both in respect to the Gnostic identification of salvation with knowledge and its dualistic vision. Although Scholem consistently makes clear his opinion that in Lurianic thought "the similarity is, of course, unintentional" (*Major Trends* 260; see also 322ff.), and while Gnostic literature was overtly anti-Semitic, there are parallels which Singer (although probably also unintentionally) often brings to the surface. See Jonas.
7. See also Buchen 198; Farrell Lee, "Seeing and Blindness" 155–57, "Conversations" 6, 17.
8. Hochman writes: "His work, to be sure, is formulated in terms of the traditional questions of evil and justice, and it leans upon a stable frame of traditional folkways to contain its vision. Yet it is suffused with the prevailing contemporary sense of isolation, disintegration, alienation, and dread, and it provides a further spice of the exotic, on the one hand, and of the transcendent solutions grounded (though ambiguously) in a primitive craving for love, on the other" (131).
9. The letter may be another play on the Kabbalistic idea of the linguistic basis of reality (see chap. 2). That there is no letter indicates that there is no divinely created world order. See discussion of "The Last Demon" above.
10. Robin McAllister, Professor of English at Sacred Heart University, points out in discussions how fond Singer seems to be of holding weddings close to gravesites. For example, see "Gimpel the Fool," whose wedding is held at the cemetery gates "near the little corpse-washing hut" (*Gimpel* 7).
11. Pondrom states that Singer's "demons or forces always manifest themselves in psychological terms" ("Interview" 18). However, my reading is more in line with Fixler's. He writes: "'The Black Wedding,' for example, is obviously written with a fine understanding of sexual hysteria, but just as clearly the subjective hallucinations of the girl in the story read like a case of demonic possession. Here as in other instances in Singer's fiction, archa-

ically primitive and sophisticated modern premises are presented as simultaneously plausible" (372).

12. See Scholem, *On the Kabbalah* 146–53.
13. "Since God wanted us to have free will this means that Satan, in other words the principle of evil, must exist. Because what does free choice mean? It means the freedom to choose between good and evil. If there is no evil there is no freedom" (Farrell Lee, "Seeing and Blindness" 157).
14. This is actually a traditional Kabbalic interpretation. As Scholem points out, "Some kabbalists maintained that the breaking [of the vessels] was not just an unfortunate accident, but a carefully planned occurrence designed to provide man with the freedom of choice between good and evil" (*Sabbatai Sevi* 35).

## 4. Mythic Dimensions of Exile: Community, Part One

1. For discussion of the *Sefer Yezirah*, see chap. 2.
2. The historical significance of community in Singer's work has been well defined by Buchen: "To Singer the family represents the Jewish community in miniature. The Jewish community in turn is the stepping-stone and basic unit of history. When the family is fragmented, the communal ties are broken and the historical analogue between the two is shattered" (90). Chametzky writes, in regard to *Satan in Goray*, "What [Singer] is concerned to do is to present within the framework of Jewish experience, perhaps within that experience above all others because it transcends the normal categories of history . . . the perennial struggle between order and chaos" (171).
3. See especially Scholem, *Sabbatai Sevi* 42.
4. For discussions of *tikkun*, see Scholem, *Kabbalah* 140–44, *On the Kabbalah* 113–17, *Messianic Idea* 184–96, *Major Trends* 278.
5. For discussions of the link between human and cosmic redemption, see Scholem, *Kabbalah* 244ff., *Messianic Idea* chaps. 1, 2.
6. Buchen explains: "To Singer Jewish reality is defined as the reality of relationships. Marriage thus serves as the most congenially artistic means of examining and judging the Jewish *shtetl*. Indeed, because in Singer's world the breakdown of marriage often involves the rejection of Jewishness, both losses become

emblematic of the larger disintegration of the community. The particular source of marital discord in Singer's works is mismatching. The short story, 'Big and Little,' as its title suggests, completely revolves about an oddly yoked couple. In *The Family Moskat,* Abram Shapiro compares his marriage to a 'square peg in a round hole.' Nyunie sums up his domestic lot in less revealing sexual terms: '"Not a wife—a plague."' In one of Singer's short stories, the Devil confesses that one of his most successful strategems is to mismatch people in marriage. . . . Couples claw at each other, castrate each other, are unfaithful, remain together to practice the special art of intimate sadism, divorce each other, and implant their sour hostilities in their children. What all these botched and blemished marriages lead to is intermarriage which at least in Singer's world is the ultimate mismatch. With that final act the individual divorces himself not only from the family, but also from God. Indeed, the image of Jewish tradition in tatters at the end of [*The Family Moskat*] finds its counterpart in the marital debris and carnage scattered throughout the novel" (38–39).

7. Eliade writes: "Since 'our world' is a cosmos, any attack from without threatens to turn it into chaos. And as 'our world' was founded by imitating the paradigmatic work of the gods, the cosmogony, so the enemies who attack it are assimilated to the enemies of the gods, the demons, and especially to the archdemon, the primordial dragon conquered by the gods at the beginning of time. An attack on 'our world' is equivalent to an act of revenge by the mythical dragon, who rebels against the work of the gods, the cosmos, and struggles to annihilate it" (47–48).
8. For an exhaustive treatment of the Sabbatian movement, see Scholem, *Sabbatai Sevi.* See also *Messianic Idea, Kabbalah* 244–84.
9. Eliade notes that "'our world'" stands in opposition to "the unknown and indeterminate space that surrounds it. . . . everything outside it is no longer a cosmos but a sort of 'other world,' a foreign, chaotic space, peopled by ghosts, demons, 'foreigners'" (29). Significantly, in "The Gentleman from Cracow" and *Satan in Goray,* the demonic and its representatives enter from outside the community.
10. Gittleman writes: "It is the town isolated from other settled

places by topography and eschatology. Its remoteness is absolute. Goray is the town on the edge, the marginal town, the town on the verge of falling into the void, the town whose existence is measured by its proximity to the cosmic cataclysm ending the world. It is *the* apocalyptic town" ("Apocalyptic Town" 69).

11. Historical parallels may be noted in Scholem, *Sabbatai Sevi* 92.
12. Scholem notes that "quarrels in the synagogue must have been frequent, particularly on the Sabbath. One unbeliever was beaten up and severely wounded on the Sabbath, and when Moses Nahmias made the pilgrimage to Gallipoli he was instructed by the believing party to inquire whether or not it was permitted to shed the blood of unbelievers who spoke contemptuously of the messiah. Sabbatai replied that this was permitted" (*Sabbatai Sevi* 505).
13. Trachtenberg also notes that "a special connection exists . . . between the storm-winds, tempests, whirlwinds, and the evil spirits" (34).
14. See the discussion of evil above, chap. 3. For a discussion of the importance of the *kelippot* in the Sabbatian movement, see Scholem, *Sabbatai Sevi* 33–50.
15. Scholem emphasizes the magnitude of this departure from previous conceptions of the *Shekhinah* (*On the Kabbalah* 104ff.).
16. See also Scholem, *On the Kabbalah* 140, 148. It should be noted that the Kabbalah maintains a unity of identity between *Ein-Sof* and the *sefirot*. However, in the personification and pictorializing of these attributes of *Ein-Sof*, this identity often is not functional.
17. A parallel may be noted in Christ's "harrowing of hell."
18. Rechele's identification with the *Shekhinah* has not been noted by other critics. Her association with community has been discussed by Buchen and mentioned by Wolkenfeld. Buchen writes that "Rechele is a portrait of the abandoned and unwed Israel, waiting for love and a bridegroom. Wed first by Mates, she tastes the impotence of asceticism. Seduced later by Gedaliya, she experiences the fruitlessness of lust. . . . Finally, just as the Jews of Goray are possessed by evil, Rechele is impregnated by Satan and carries within her womb a blaspheming dubbuk" (95).

    Wolkenfeld notes, "Indeed [Rechele] remains as an image of

Goray, the community tortured by its position in history, by its desire for a meaningful spiritual life, by an inner, perhaps unavoidable, weakness" (354). For other readings, see Knopp 30–44; Gittleman, "Apocalyptic Town"; Malkoff; Milfull.

19. For a full description of Sarah, see Scholem, *Sabbatai Sevi* chap. 2.
20. See Trachtenberg, 146–49. "The mezuzah . . . retained its original significance as an amulet despite rabbinic efforts to make it an exclusively religious symbol" (146).
21. For Sabbatai's identification with Shaddai, see Scholem, *Sabbatai Sevi* 234; for discussion of Habillo, see 173.

**5. Historical and Personal Dimensions of Exile: Community, Part Two**

1. See chap. 2, 19–20 for a discussion of the significance of letters and prayer in Hasidism.
2. See Buchen for an excellent treatment of the historical significance of community throughout Singer's long fiction. For a fine analysis of *The Manor,* see Ellmann. For other noteworthy commentaries on the novels, see Alexander; Bezanker; Knopp; Ben Siegel.
3. See chap. 6, 96 for further discussion of this passage.
4. Buchen notes that the original Yiddish version does not end with these words but continues for eleven more pages (81, note 21).
5. Most discussions of Shosha treat her more realistically than I am here suggesting and then become bogged down with the problem of Aaron's motivation in loving her. If she is treated allegorically, the book succeeds aesthetically.
6. See chap. 3, 52, 53.
7. For a full treatment of the magician in folk religion, see Trachtenberg.
8. The overall pattern of the novel and its alternating design of sacred and profane spaces has not been noted by other critics, although Pondrom, "Conjuring Reality," and Knopp discuss some of the prayerhouse scenes.
9. Most discussions of the ending of *The Magician of Lublin* conclude that after a life of total freedom, Yasha pulls back to a life of utmost restriction. The critical literature stresses Yasha's sin-

fulness and discusses the efficacy of his repentance. Buchen adds that Yasha's punishment may "serve as the threshold for genuine freedom and expression" (112). Wolkenfeld states that "freedom ultimately becomes a trap like any other" (355) and views the conclusion as a positive vision of Yasha's embrace of faith. Knopp also reads Yasha's imprisonment as a positive act of conversion, while Pondrom discusses the ending of the novel with more skepticism, suggesting that it may be "a closing of his eyes" to the difficult ambiguities of life ("Conjuring Reality" 107).

Singer's ethical perspective on Yasha is made quite clear in the novel—the magician's licentious behavior is cruelly destructive. But that behavior masks what is at the heart of the novel—Yasha's search for meaning. The focus of the work is not on sin and retribution but on the spiritual torment of a human being exiled in a world which does not provide clear answers to what life is about and how it might be lived.

See also Howe; Chametzky.

# *Bibliography*

Alexander, Edward. *Isaac Bashevis Singer.* Boston: Twayne, 1980.

Allentuck, Marcia, ed. *The Achievement of Isaac Bashevis Singer.* Carbondale: Southern Illinois UP, 1969.

Ben-Amos, Dan, and Jerome R. Mintz. *In Praise of the Baal Shem Tov.* Bloomington: U of Indiana P, 1972.

Bezanker, Abraham. "I. B. Singer's Crises of Identity." *Critique* 14 (1972): 70–88.

Bloom, Harold. *Kabbalah and Criticism.* New York: Seabury, 1975.

Buber, Martin. *The Origin and Meaning of Hasidism.* New York: Harper, 1960.

———. *Tales of the Hasidim.* 2 vols. New York: Schocken, 1948.

———. *The Tales of Rabbi Nachman.* Bloomington: U of Indiana P, 1956.

Buchen, Irving H. *Isaac Bashevis Singer. and the Eternal Past.* New York: New York UP, 1968.

Burgin, Richard. "The Sly Modernism of Isaac Singer." *Chicago Review* 31 (1980): 61–67.

Camus, Albert. "An Absurd Reasoning." *The Myth of Sisyphus.* New York: Random, 1955.

Chametzky, Jules. "History in I. B. Singer's Novels." Malin 169–77.

Eliade, Mircea. *The Sacred and the Profane.* New York: Harcourt, 1959.

Ellmann, Mary. "The Piety of Things in *The Manor.*" Allentuck 124–44.

Farrell Lee, Grace. "Conversations with the Singers. *Sacred Heart University Review* 1 (1981): 3–18.

———. "Seeing and Blindness: A Conversation with Isaac Bashevis Singer." *Novel* 9 (1976): 151–64.

Fixler, Michael. "The Redeemers: Themes in the Fiction of Isaac Bashevis Singer." *Kenyon Review* 26 (1964): 371–86.

Franck, Adolphe. *The Kabbalah*. New York: Bell, 1960.

Friedman, Maurice. *Problematic Rebel*. Chicago: U of Chicago P, 1973.

Gaster, Theodore H. *The Dead Sea Scriptures*. New York: Anchor, 1956.

Gittleman, Edwin. "Dybbukianism: The Meaning of Method in Singer's Short Stories." *Contemporary American-Jewish Literature*. Ed. Irving Malin. Bloomington: U of Indiana P, 1973. 248–69.

———. "Singer's Apocalyptic Town: *Satan in Goray*." Allentuck 64–76.

Glanville, Brian. "An Interview with Isaac Bashevis Singer." *The Jewish Notes* 28 Sept. 1962: 28.

Hochman, Baruch. "Singer's Vision of Good and Evil." Malin 120–34.

Howe, Irving. "Demonic Fiction of a Yiddish Modernist." *Commentary* Oct. 1960: 350–53.

Jonas, Hans. *The Gnostic Religion*. Boston: Beacon, 1963.

Knopp, Josephine. *The Trial of Judaism in Contemporary Jewish Writing*. Urbana: U of Illinois P, 1975.

Krieger, Murray. *The Tragic Vision*. Baltimore: Johns Hopkins UP, 1973.

Maimonides, Moses. *The Guide of the Perplexed*. Trans. Shlomo Pines. Chicago: U of Chicago P, 1974.

Malin, Irving, ed. *Critical Views of Isaac Bashevis Singer*. New York: New York UP, 1965.

Malkoff, Karl. "Demonology and Dualism: The Supernatural in Isaac Singer and Muriel Spark." Malin 149–68.

Milfull, John. "The Messiah and the Direction of History: Walter Benjamin, Isaac Bashevis Singer, and Franz Kafka." In *Festschrift for E. W. Herd*. Ed. August Obermayer and T. E. Carter. Dunedin, N.Z.: German Department, University of Otago, 1980. 180–87.

Pinsker, Sanford. "The Fictive Worlds of Isaac Bashevis

Singer." *Critique: Studies in Modern Fiction* 2 (1969): 26–39.

Pondrom, Cyrena N. "Conjuring Reality: I. B. Singer's *The Magician of Lublin.*" Allentuck 93–111.

———. "Isaac Bashevis Singer: An Interview." *Contemporary Literature* 10 (1969): 1–32.

Ricoeur, Paul. *The Symbolism of Evil.* Boston: Beacon, 1969.

Riddel, Joseph N. "Review Article on Harold Bloom." *Georgia Review* 30 (1976): 989–1006.

Sachar, Howard Morley. *The Course of Modern Jewish History.* New York: Delta, 1958.

Schaya, Leo. *The Universal Meaning of the Kabbalah.* Baltimore: Penguin, 1973.

Scholem, Gershom. *Kabbalah.* New York: NAL, 1978.

———. *Major Trends in Jewish Mysticism.* New York: Schocken, 1954.

———. *The Messianic Idea in Judaism.* New York: Schocken, 1971.

———. "The Name of God and the Linguistic Theory of the Kabbala." *Diogenes* 79 (1972): 59–80, 80 (1972): 164–94.

———. *On the Kabbalah and Its Symbolism.* New York: Schocken, 1969.

———. *Sabbatai Sevi.* Princeton: Princeton UP, 1973.

———. "Schöpfung aus Nichts und Selbstverschränkung Gottes." *Eranos Yearbook* 25 (1957): 87–119.

———. *Zohar.* New York: Schocken, 1975.

Siegel, Ben. *Isaac Bashevis Singer.* Minneapolis: U of Minnesota P, 1969.

Siegel, Paul N. "Gimpel and the Archetype of the Wise Fool." Allentuck 159–74.

Singer, Isaac Bashevis. *"A Crown of Feathers" and Other Stories.* New York: Farrar, 1973.

———. *Enemies, A Love Story.* New York: Farrar, 1972.

———. *The Estate.* New York: Farrar, 1969.

———. *The Family Moskat.* New York: Farrar, 1965.

———. *"A Friend of Kafka" and Other Stories.* New York: Farrar, 1970.

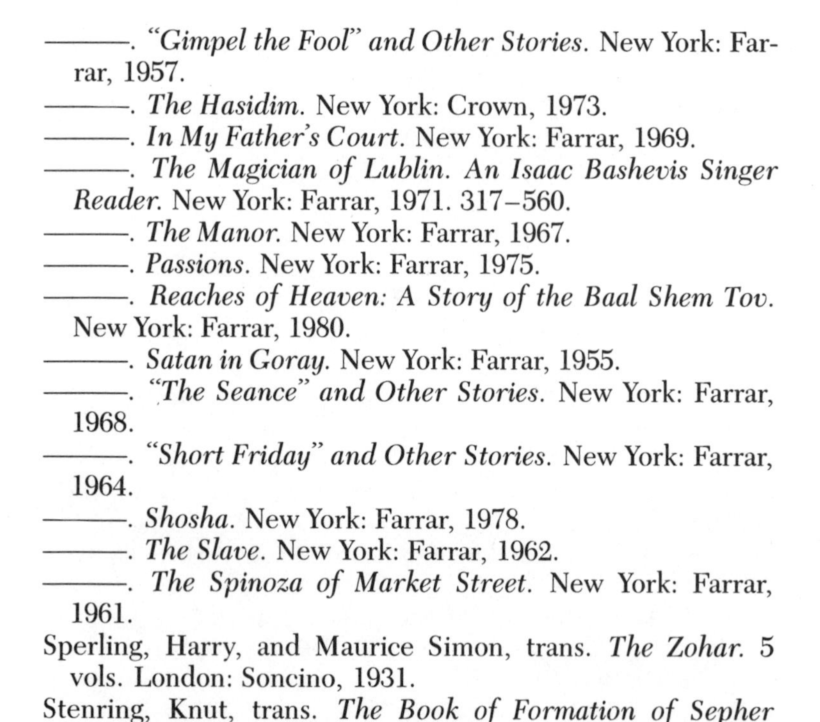

———. *"Gimpel the Fool" and Other Stories*. New York: Farrar, 1957.

———. *The Hasidim*. New York: Crown, 1973.

———. *In My Father's Court*. New York: Farrar, 1969.

———. *The Magician of Lublin. An Isaac Bashevis Singer Reader*. New York: Farrar, 1971. 317–560.

———. *The Manor*. New York: Farrar, 1967.

———. *Passions*. New York: Farrar, 1975.

———. *Reaches of Heaven: A Story of the Baal Shem Tov*. New York: Farrar, 1980.

———. *Satan in Goray*. New York: Farrar, 1955.

———. *"The Seance" and Other Stories*. New York: Farrar, 1968.

———. *"Short Friday" and Other Stories*. New York: Farrar, 1964.

———. *Shosha*. New York: Farrar, 1978.

———. *The Slave*. New York: Farrar, 1962.

———. *The Spinoza of Market Street*. New York: Farrar, 1961.

Sperling, Harry, and Maurice Simon, trans. *The Zohar*. 5 vols. London: Soncino, 1931.

Stenring, Knut, trans. *The Book of Formation of Sepher Yetzirah*. By Rabbi Akiba Ben Joseph. London: William Rider, 1923.

Trachtenberg, Joshua. *Jewish Magic and Superstitution*. New York: Atheneum, 1975.

Wisse, Ruth R. *The Schlemiel as Modern Hero*. Chicago: U of Chicago P, 1971.

Wolkenfeld, J. S. "Isaac Bashevis Singer: The Faith of His Devils and Magicians." *Criticism* 5 (1963): 349–59.

# Index

GRACE FARRELL LEE holds M.A. and Ph.D. degrees from Brown University and is Professor of English at a college in Connecticut. Author of numerous essays and reviews on nineteenth and twentieth century fiction, she was awarded a Fellowship from the National Endowment for the Humanities to write *From Exile to Redemption: The Fiction of Isaac Bashevis Singer.*